Mara the Meerkat Fairy

Special thanks to Narinder Dhami

No part of this work may be reproduced, stored in a retrieval system, or transmitted in any form or by any means, electronic, mechanical, photocopying, recording, or otherwise, without written permission of the publisher. For information regarding permission, write to Rainbow Magic Limited c/o HIT Entertainment, 830 South Greenville Avenue, Allen, TX 75002-3320.

ISBN 978-0-545-70850-0

12 11 10 9 8 7 6 5 4 3 2 1   15 16 17 18 19/0

Printed in the U.S.A.   40

First Scholastic printing, January 2015

Mara
the Meerkat
Fairy

by Daisy Meadows

SCHOLASTIC INC.

The Fairyland Palace

Meadow

Stream

Beehive

Arctic Tundra

Eucalyptus Forest

Tropical Waterfall

Jack Frost's
Ice Castle

Wild Woods
Nature
Reserve

To Jack Frost's Zoo

Watering Hole

Pagoda

Desert Oasis

I love animals—yes, I do,
I want my very own private zoo!
I'll capture all the animals one by one,
With fairy magic to help me get it done!

A koala, a tiger, an Arctic fox,
I'll keep them in cages with giant locks.
Every kind of animal will be there,
A panda, a meerkat, a honey bear.
The animals will be my property,
I'll be master of my own menagerie!

Contents

A Very Tricky Task

"So, all we know about today's job is that it's going to be especially tricky!" Kirsty Tate remarked to her best friend, Rachel Walker, as they made their way along a path through the woods.

The two girls had volunteered to spend a week of summer vacation working as junior rangers at Wild Woods Nature Reserve. "What do you think we'll be doing, Rachel?"

"I don't know, but I'm looking forward to finding out when we meet Becky in the meadow!" Rachel replied with a grin. Becky was the head of the nature reserve. "I hope it's something we can do really well—and then we *might* earn another badge."

"I *love* getting badges," Kirsty said happily. She swung her backpack off her shoulders so she could proudly sneak a peek at the badges pinned to the pockets. This was the girls' third day at Wild Woods, and they'd already earned two badges because they'd successfully completed their tasks on the previous two days.

The girls heard a rustling noise in the undergrowth, and a little red squirrel scampered out of the bushes. He stopped

2

in front of Rachel and Kirsty and gave
them a mischievous glance.

"I heard what you were saying," the
squirrel told them breathlessly. "And,
you're right: You'll have a very difficult
job to do today!" Then, giggling, he
bounded away.

"Good luck!" chirped a voice from above. The girls looked up and saw a pair of goldfinches  sitting on a branch side by side. "Like the squirrel said, you've got a very tricky task today."

"Very tricky!" the other goldfinch agreed. Then the two birds soared up into the blue sky.

"It's such amazing fun being able to talk to animals!" Rachel exclaimed. "We couldn't do it without the Baby Animal Rescue Fairies' magic."

Kirsty nodded. "I just wish we hadn't

been given this magic for such a serious reason." She sighed. "We need the power to talk to animals so we can save wildlife everywhere from scary Jack Frost and his goblins!"

Rachel and Kirsty were in the middle of another thrilling fairy adventure. On their first day at Wild Woods, they'd met Bertram, a frog footman from Fairyland who was visiting relatives at the nature reserve. At Bertram's invitation, the girls had been taken on a tour of the Fairyland Nature Reserve where they'd met the Baby Animal Rescue Fairies. These seven fairies were responsible for protecting animals in both the human and the fairy worlds. They all wore special animal key chains clipped to their clothing, and they used the magic in the charms to help them.

Then Jack Frost and his goblins had arrived to spoil the girls' special day! Jack Frost had declared that he liked all the animals so much, he was going to collect one of each for his private zoo. He'd used his icy magic to steal the key chains. The girls had been horrified when Jack Frost had then thrown the charms to his goblins and sent them to the human world, ordering them to bring back animals for his zoo.

The seven fairies were very upset, and the girls had offered their help. Immediately, the fairies had combined their magic, giving Rachel and Kirsty the ability to talk to animals.

"So far we've met a baby panda and three tiger cubs," Rachel reminded

Kirsty as they approached the meadow. "I wonder if we'll meet another wild animal today?"

"There's Becky," Kirsty said, peering across the meadow. "Look, Rachel, she has a wheelbarrow with her."

Becky saw the girls and waved.

"Becky's not alone in the meadow!" Rachel said with a grin, and she pointed at a rabbit hopping across the grass.

"There's another rabbit over there!"
Kirsty exclaimed. "And there's another—
and another!"

By the time Rachel and Kirsty had
climbed over the fence into the meadow,
they'd already spotted eight rabbits
hopping around. Quickly, the girls ran to
join Becky. She was standing next to the
wheelbarrow and they saw it was full of
carrots, lettuce, and cabbage leaves.

"Good morning, Rachel and Kirsty," Becky said, her eyes twinkling. "Your job for today is to count rabbits!"

Rachel looked at Kirsty with alarm. That *did* sound like a difficult job!

Bunny Bother!

"I know it sounds silly," Becky went on, "but it's very useful for us to know the size of the rabbit population at Wild Woods. It helps us take care of the environment and the animals properly." She handed clipboards and pens to the girls. "Every time you see a rabbit, write it down," Becky went on. "You can use these veggies in the wheelbarrow to tempt the rabbits out of their burrows." She pointed to the holes that the rabbits had dug in the meadow.

"We'll do our best," Kirsty promised.

"Good luck!" Becky told them. "I'll be back later to see how you're doing." She hurried off.

"There are lots of rabbits here!" Rachel remarked as a big brown bunny hopped past them. "They're all different sizes and colors."

"Some are just babies, too," Kirsty added. "I've got a feeling this is going to take us all day! Should we count the bunnies in the field first?"

"Good idea," Rachel replied.

The girls ran around the meadow, counting all the rabbits they could see, keeping a tally on their clipboards. It was hard work because the rabbits wouldn't stay still, and kept hopping all over the place.

"I wonder how many rabbits are in the holes," Rachel panted as she and Kirsty set the carrots, lettuce, and cabbage leaves on the grass in front of the burrows. Then the girls stood by, clipboards at the ready. Soon furry heads began popping out of the holes, and rabbit after rabbit came hopping out, heading straight for the tasty vegetables.

"Ten, eleven, twelve!" Kirsty gasped as yet another rabbit scampered out of the burrow next to her. "There are tons

14

of them, Rachel! And look—more are
coming out of those holes that are a little
farther away."

"I'll count those," Rachel suggested.
"It'll be easier." And she hurried off,
muttering, "Fourteen, fifteen, sixteen,
seventeen . . ."

Kirsty didn't have a second to spare as
she frantically counted the bunnies and
then marked the number down on her
clipboard. A short
distance away,
Rachel was doing
the same. The
vegetables were
running out now, so
Kirsty raced over to
the wheelbarrow
to grab some more.

The rabbits were munching away contentedly and Kirsty was counting under her breath when a small brown bunny hopped over to her.

"Excuse me," the bunny squeaked. "But have you counted *me* yet?"

"Yes, I just did." Kirsty laughed.

"Oh, dear!" The rabbit sighed. "Your friend counted me already."

"Are you sure?" Kirsty asked, her heart sinking.

"Yes, she said I was number thirty-five!" the bunny replied.

Two more rabbits looked up from their lettuce leaves. "Your friend counted me already, too," one said.

"And me!" the other added.

"Oh, no!" Kirsty groaned. She'd added these rabbits to her clipboard just a moment ago!

"Rachel?" Kirsty called, looking worried. "Some of the rabbits are telling me we *both* counted them!"

"Yes, a rabbit has just told me the exact same thing," Rachel replied, rushing over to Kirsty.

The girls were disappointed, but they couldn't help giggling.

"This isn't just a tricky task!" Kirsty laughed. "It's impossible!"

"Should we start all over again?" asked Rachel.

"I think the same thing will happen again," Kirsty replied. "Maybe we need a better plan."

The girls watched the rabbits for a few moments, wondering how they could count them without getting confused. Kirsty focused on one baby bunny who had a cute, fuzzy bit of fur sticking up on top of his head. The baby rabbit disappeared down a nearby hole. Then, just seconds later, Kirsty gasped when the same rabbit popped out of a *different* hole a little farther away.

"Rachel, I know why we've been getting confused!" Kirsty exclaimed. "I think the rabbits are going down one hole and then popping out of another. That's why we're counting them twice."

"I saw a TV show about meerkats once, and they lived underground in a maze of tunnels," Rachel said thoughtfully. "I bet these holes lead to lots of tunnels under the meadow, and *that's* how the bunnies can run around and pop in and out of different holes so easily."

Kirsty nodded. "We need a different way of counting them," she said, staring down at the rabbit burrow. That's when

she noticed a misty golden glow around
the entrance of the hole.

"I think I see fairy magic!" Kirsty
announced excitedly, pointing at the
glowing light.

The two girls raced over to investigate. As they reached the rabbit hole, a fairy fluttered out to greet them.

"You're Mara the Meerkat Fairy!" Rachel gasped.

On Guard Against Goblins

Mara's anxious face broke into a smile. The little fairy wore a maroon and orange polka-dot dress with a narrow brown belt, leggings, and purple Mary Jane flats.

"Girls, I desperately need your help to protect a colony of my meerkats!" Mara cried. "The meerkat guards have spotted goblins near their burrow."

"Let's go right away!" Kirsty said.
Quickly, she and Rachel put their
clipboards in their backpacks. Mara was
ready with her wand, and one sprinkling
of magical fairy dust instantly whisked
the three of them away from the nature
reserve.

Just a few seconds later the girls found
themselves standing on top of a huge
sand dune, the burning sun beating down
from a cloudless sky. A vast desert of

dazzling orange sand stretched out around them, and the only objects Kirsty and Rachel could see were some half dead, leafless trees in the distance.

"I can't see any meerkats!" Rachel began, turning around to look. But the sand was slippery underfoot, and she lost her balance. Rachel gasped as she fell backward. The next thing she knew, she was sliding down the slope on her back.

"That's one way to get down the sand dune, I guess!" Mara laughed, fluttering after her.

Once Rachel had gotten over the shock, she started enjoying herself as she tumbled down, sending sand flying around her. Kirsty laughed as she sat down, and then slid along the sandy slope behind Rachel.

Giggling, the girls landed in a heap at the bottom of the dune.

"That was a lot of fun!" Rachel panted, standing up. "But now I'm really hot and thirsty."

"We have water in our backpacks," Kirsty reminded her. "And sunscreen."

"You'll need both to stay safe in this heat, girls," said Mara.

The girls drank some water, then they covered themselves with the sunscreen.

"That's better," Rachel remarked. "But I still don't see any meerkats!"

Mara laughed. "The desert is full of them," she replied. "Just use your eyes!"

The girls glanced around. They both caught sight of something moving in a hole in the sand and crept closer. Then a furry little head popped out.

"It's a baby meerkat!"
Kirsty exclaimed.

"Oh, she's
so cute!"
Rachel
whispered in
awe, staring at
the meerkat's black-
ringed eyes and tiny black ears.

Suddenly, the baby meerkat was
pulled gently back down the hole, and
two adult meerkats scampered out.
Immediately, they sat up on their back
legs and began scanning the desert all
around them. Then the girls saw the
baby meerkat poke her head out again.
She waved and smiled at Rachel and
Kirsty, her dark eyes bright and playful.
The girls were enchanted.

"Isn't she gorgeous?" Kirsty said as she and Rachel smiled and waved back.

"Girls, meet Missy, short for Mischief!" Mara said, pointing her wand at the baby meerkat. "These other two are our brave meerkat guards."

"We're glad to see you, Mara," one of the guards squeaked. "There have been some *very* strange green creatures with big feet wandering around the desert."

Rachel glanced knowingly at Kirsty. *Goblins!*

"The other meerkats are staying underground out of sight until those funny green animals leave," the other guard added. "We really don't like them!"

Just then the girls heard noises in the distance. The meerkat guards heard them, too, and their whiskers started twitching nervously.

The noises were coming closer, and Kirsty could make out the sound of loud, gruff voices.

"Goblins!" She gasped.

Squeaking with anxiety, the meerkat guards dove for the hole and disappeared down it with Missy.

"Girls, let's try to keep the goblins from coming any closer," Mara whispered, flying to hide beneath Kirsty's sun hat.

Swiftly, Rachel and Kirsty hurried across the sand in the direction of the voices. Then they saw three goblins wearing bright green shorts, shirts, and large sun hats stagger over the top of a nearby dune. They all looked sweaty and exhausted.

"I'm too hot!" the smallest goblin wailed miserably.

"Stop complaining!" the biggest goblin retorted. "We can go as soon as we find a meerkat to take with us."

"But where *are* the meerkats?" asked the third goblin, who had extra-large ears. "We haven't seen any yet."

As the girls approached the goblins, Rachel gasped and clutched Kirsty's arm. "Look at the biggest goblin's shorts!" she whispered.

Kirsty stared at the side pocket of the goblin's shorts, and Mara peeked out from her hiding place to take a look, too. They could see a small, furry meerkat charm sticking out.

"That's my magic key chain!" Mara murmured with a smile.

"Good! Now we know exactly where it is," Kirsty said. "But how do we get it back?"

Mara frowned and crossed her arms. "I'm not sure, but we have to think of something quickly!"

Missy Makes Mischief!

The goblins trudged on through the sand, grumbling loudly about the heat. When they reached the girls, they stopped.

"Are there meerkats around here?" the smallest goblin asked hopefully.

Kirsty laughed. "There are no meerkats in the desert!" she replied with a grin.

"The only meerkat around here is that cute little toy," Rachel remarked casually, pointing at Mara's key chain poking out of the goblin's pocket.

The biggest goblin groaned and took off his hat to wipe his sweaty green brow. The other two did the same, and that gave Kirsty an idea.

"It's really hot, isn't it?" she said
sympathetically. "Don't you have any
water to cool down?"

"We did, but we drank it all," the
smallest goblin replied.

"Well, Rachel and I have plenty,"
Kirsty said. She took a bottle of water
from her backpack, and so did Rachel.
The goblins stared greedily at the bottles,
licking their lips. "We'll trade you a
drink of our water for that
toy you have in your
pocket. Deal?"

"Deal!" the
biggest goblin
agreed instantly.
He grabbed the
water from Kirsty and
began gulping it down.

Rachel handed her bottle to the smallest goblin, who took a long drink.

"My turn!" the big-eared goblin hollered, snatching it from him.

A few moments later the goblins finished drinking and, looking much happier, they gave the bottles back to the girls.

"Now let's go and find some meerkats!" the biggest goblin shouted.

"Wait!" Kirsty said firmly. "What about our deal? You promised us your little toy meerkat."

"We can't give it to you," the biggest goblin snapped. "No way! We need it to catch a meerkat for Jack Frost."

"He'll be very angry with us if we don't bring him one for his zoo!" the smallest goblin added.

Rachel and Kirsty exchanged frustrated glances.

"I told you, there *aren't* any meerkats in the desert," Kirsty said. "You're wasting your time."

The goblins looked uncertain.

"Maybe she's right," the biggest goblin murmured. "After all, we haven't seen any meerkats yet and we've been walking for *hours*!"

"I don't think you're looking in the right place," Rachel remarked, straight-faced. "Don't you know meerkats are *cats*? They've probably climbed those trees to hide!" She pointed at the trees in the distance.

"Yes, *everyone* knows meerkats are cats!" The smallest goblin sneered.

The girls tried not to smile.

"Come on!" the big-eared goblin yelled, and the three of them hurried off toward the trees.

"Well done, girls," Mara whispered
from under Kirsty's hat. "You got them
to head away from the meerkats. Now
let's follow them and try to get my key
chain back."

But just then the biggest goblin
accidentally caught his foot in one of the
meerkat holes.

He yelped and
tripped, ending
up flat on his
face. Then,
horrified,
Kirsty saw
Missy peek
out of another
hole very close
to the goblin
who had fallen.

"Oh, no!" Kirsty said anxiously.

The girls waved their hands at Missy, trying to warn her to stay out of sight. They didn't want to call out and attract the goblins' attention.

But the biggest goblin had already spotted the baby meerkat. His eyes lit up.

"Come back!" he yelled to the other goblins, who were ahead of him. "I found a meerkat!"

Rachel and Kirsty were full of dismay as the other two goblins scurried back to join their friend. But before the goblins reached him, Missy popped out of sight again. The girls breathed heartfelt sighs of relief.

"Where's the meerkat?" the smallest goblin panted.

"It was *there*!" The biggest goblin pointed at the hole.

The other goblins frowned.

"That hole's empty." The smallest goblin snorted. "I think you're seeing things! This hot sun can play tricks on your brain, you know."

"He doesn't *have* a brain!" The goblin with huge ears giggled.

"That's not funny!" the biggest goblin snarled, looking angry.

Then Rachel and Kirsty saw a flash of brown fur inside a different hole very close by. Missy peeked out of it and stared at the goblins. They were right in front of her.

"Oh, no!" Rachel groaned. "The goblins are bound to catch little Missy this time!"

But the goblins were still arguing about whether the biggest goblin had seen a meerkat or not, and they didn't notice that there was, in fact, one right under their noses! Then, as the girls watched, Missy snuck out of the hole and grabbed Mara's magic key chain right out of the biggest goblin's pocket.

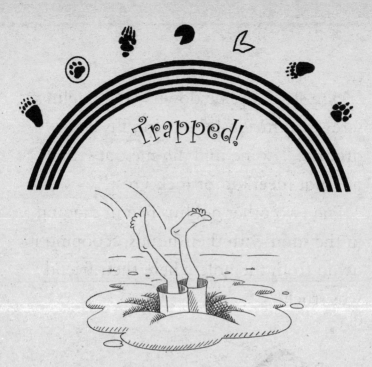

Trapped!

The girls could hardly believe their eyes.

"Missy, bring the charm to us!" Kirsty called. But Missy immediately vanished down the hole again.

The biggest goblin shrieked with rage. "Give that back, you naughty meerkat!" he shouted, and he dove headfirst into the hole. He disappeared up to his knees, but then stopped.

"I'm stuck upside down!" the goblin screeched furiously, waving his feet around. "Come and dig me out—and get that meerkat for Jack Frost!"

The two other goblins began digging in the sand with their hands, scooping it away from the hole where their friend was stuck.

"Can you see the meerkat?" the smallest goblin cried.

"No!" the biggest goblin roared.
"There are lots and lots of tunnels down
here. It's like a maze. Keep digging!"

Mara flew out from under Kirsty's hat.
"I'll turn you into fairies, girls, and then
we can fly through the tunnels and find
Missy," she told them.

One flick of Mara's wand sent
glittering fairy sparkles spinning all
around Rachel and Kirsty, shrinking
them to fairy-size. Delicate fairy wings
magically appeared on their backs. Then
Mara zoomed toward a nearby hole, and
Rachel and Kirsty flew after her.

"You know animals love our magic
key chains," Mara reminded the girls as
they entered the hole. "So we have to
find Missy and persuade her to give it
back to me. Come on, girls!"

But the instant Mara, Rachel, and Kirsty flew inside the hole, the walls of the tunnel began to shake with a loud noise. *BOOM! BOOM! BOOM!*

"What's that?" Rachel gasped nervously, dodging a clump of dirt that fell from the roof of the tunnel. Another clump tumbled down and almost hit Mara, who managed to fly out of the way just in time.

"I think the goblins must be stomping on the ground, trying to drive the meerkats out of their holes," Mara exclaimed. "We have to find Missy before the tunnels start collapsing!"

Rachel and Kirsty quickly followed Mara down the tunnel, trying to avoid the chunks of the roof and walls that were now falling around them. Kirsty couldn't believe how many passageways there were underneath the desert sand. Everywhere she looked, there were more and more tunnels going in lots of different directions.

"How do we know which way to go next?" Kirsty shouted above the noise the goblins were making.

Suddenly, the two meerkat guards came scurrying toward them.

"Have you seen Missy?" Rachel asked, looking worried.

"She went that way," one of the

meerkat guards
replied,
pointing down
a nearby
tunnel.

"We'll
deal with the
goblins as soon
as we've found
Missy and my magic
key chain," Mara promised the guards,
and she and the girls flew off.

Suddenly, a scared little voice floated
faintly up the tunnel toward them.
"Help! Help!"

"It's Missy!" Mara cried. She flew
faster, Rachel and Kirsty right at her
heels. The three friends zoomed around
the corner of the tunnel, then came to a

dead stop. There in front of them was the upside-down goblin. They'd almost flown straight into his head! It was blocking the tunnel!

Then Rachel yelped in dismay. She'd spotted Missy on the other side of the goblin. The baby meerkat, still clutching Mara's magic charm, was cowering away from the goblin. Beyond Missy, Rachel could see that the tunnel had collapsed because of the goblins stomping around overhead. Missy couldn't go forward because of the goblin, and she couldn't go backward because of the blocked tunnel.

"Missy's trapped!" Rachel cried. "And so is Mara's magic key chain!"

Rabbit Lineup

The upside-down goblin was staring at
Mara and the girls.

"Go away!" he shouted. "You can't
have that magic key chain—it's mine,
and so is this meerkat!"

Missy whimpered in distress.

"Rachel, you help Missy escape,"
Mara whispered. "Kirsty and I will try to
distract the goblin by tickling him!"

Rachel flew as close to the goblin as she dared. "Missy, don't be frightened," she called. "Just come over here to me. I promise you'll be safe."

"Don't you dare move!" the goblin screeched at Missy. "I want that magic key chain, and you're coming with me to Jack Frost's zoo!"

"Let's go, Kirsty!" Mara whispered. The two of them zoomed over to the goblin and, fluttering around him, they began tickling his ribs.

"Stop that!" the goblin yelled. "*Ha-ha, hee-hee*—no, stop it! *Ha-ha-ha!*"

Rachel beckoned to Missy, who
stepped forward cautiously. There was
only a small gap between the goblin and
the wall of the tunnel, but Missy bravely
began squeezing through the small space.
Rachel watched, her heart pounding.

But then, just as Missy climbed over
the goblin's arm to safety, his hand shot
out and he yanked the magic charm
away from her.

"Your silly plan didn't work!" The
goblin gloated triumphantly as Missy
scrambled past him to the other side of
the tunnel. "I've got the key chain back!
Aren't I smart?"

"You're not that smart, really," Kirsty
pointed out. "After all, you're still stuck
in the sand!"

"But we'll help you out of the hole if

you give us my meerkat key chain back,"
Mara added.

The goblin's face fell. "So *either* I go
back to Jack Frost's Ice Castle without a
meerkat, *or* I stay stuck upside down in
the desert?" he asked sulkily.

"You decide!" Rachel told him.

The goblin scowled. Then reluctantly
he held out the key chain to Mara. "Help
me!" he muttered.

Smiling delightedly, Mara touched her
magic key chain and it
immediately shrank
to its Fairyland
size. Quickly, Mara
clipped it to her belt.

"Come on, girls," she
said. "We'll have to go outside again to
free the goblin."

The three friends flew back along the tunnels toward the hole, a curious Missy scampering along behind.

"The other goblins have stopped stomping around," Rachel remarked as they flew out of the hole. "I wonder why?" Then she smiled as she saw the two goblins lying exhausted on the sand.

"Look, there's a meerkat," the smallest goblin said

wearily, pointing at Missy.

"I don't care!" the goblin with the big ears wailed. "I've never been so hot and tired in my entire life!"

Mara pointed her wand at the biggest goblin's feet sticking out of the sand. On the count of one, he shot out of the hole backward, like a ball from a cannon. He landed safely near the other two.

"Poor old goblins!" Mara said. "They look really tired, don't they?"

She waved her wand again, and the girls saw a pool of clear water, surrounded by tall palm trees, appear nearby.

"It's an oasis!" the biggest goblin exclaimed. "Yay!"

The three goblins raced over to the oasis and began gulping down water in the cool shade. Rachel and Kirsty grinned at each other.

"My magic has repaired all the underground tunnels, too," Mara explained to the girls.

Rachel and Kirsty could now see Missy and the other meerkats popping out of all the holes. "Thank you!" the meerkats squeaked. "Thank you for protecting us."

"And thank *you* for all your help, girls," Mara said. "I couldn't have done it without you. How thrilled they'll be in Fairyland when I give them the good news! And now it's time for you to return to Wild Woods."

"Good-bye, Missy," Rachel and Kirsty called as Mara lifted her wand for the third time. "Good-bye, Mara!"

A mist of fairy sparkles dazzled the girls for a moment. Then they found themselves in the meadow again, human-size and surrounded by rabbits.

"I have an idea how we can count the

rabbits," Kirsty announced. She checked to make sure no one was around, then she turned to a group of bunnies. "Excuse me," Kirsty said, "would you mind lining up so we can count you?"

"Of course we don't mind!" the rabbits agreed, and they hopped to stand together in a tidy line. The girls hurried around the field, asking all the other bunnies to join them. Soon they had a long, long line winding all around the meadow.

"That was a fantastic idea, Kirsty!" Rachel exclaimed as they counted the last few rabbits. "Well, that makes fifty-two in all."

"Not quite," Kirsty replied, smiling as a baby bunny scurried over to join the end of the line. "Fifty-three!"

"Thank you, bunnies!" Rachel called, and then the girls saw Becky coming through the woods. The rabbits immediately scattered.

"Just in time!" Kirsty whispered.

"How did things go, girls?" Becky inquired, coming to join them.

"Oh, we counted a total of fifty-three rabbits in this meadow," Kirsty said confidently, and she and Rachel showed Becky their clipboards.

"Nice work, girls," Becky said with

a smile. "I'm impressed. It was a very tricky task—and I really think you earned your badges!" She handed them a badge each, and the girls were thrilled to see that they had a picture of a rabbit on them.

"Wasn't Missy adorable?" Kirsty whispered as she and Rachel followed Becky back to the nature center.

"She was cuter than cute!" Rachel whispered back. "And I can't *wait* to find out which animals we'll be meeting tomorrow!"

Rachel and Kirsty found Mae, Kitty,
and Mara's missing magic key chains.
Now it's time for them to help

Savannah
the Zebra Fairy!

Join their next adventure in this special
sneak peek . . .

A Deer Display

"I wonder what junior ranger badges we'll earn today," said Rachel Walker as she got out of the car at the Wild Woods Nature Reserve.

"I hope we'll be spending time with the animals again," said her best friend Kirsty Tate. "Since the fairies gave us the gift of being able to understand what animals say, I want to be with them all the time!"

"Look, there's Becky," said Kirsty, seeing the head of the reserve walking toward them. "Come on, let's find out what she wants us to do today."

The girls waved good-bye to Mrs. Tate, who had driven them to the nature reserve.

"Good morning, girls!" said Becky. "I've got an exciting job for you. I want you to feed our herd of deer. They're some of the sweetest animals on the reserve, and there's a baby fawn that's especially cute. But he's very shy, so you might not see him."

The girls could hardly believe their ears. The beautiful deer were one of the main visitor attractions at the reserve.

"Really?" Rachel gasped. "Thank you, Becky!"

"It's like a dream come true!" said Kirsty.

"Well, let's get started, then!" said Becky with a laugh.

She led the girls over to where four large buckets were waiting on the ground.

"These are full of deer feed," said Becky.

"What do the deer eat?" asked Kirsty, looking into the buckets.

"It's a special mixture of fruit and grasses," Becky told them.

Carrying two buckets each, the girls followed Becky to a pretty meadow, full of clover and buttercups. On the far side of the meadow was a leafy forest, and a fence surrounded the other three sides. There were lots of people standing beside the fence. They looked excited and hopeful.

"Look, the visitors are gathering already," said Becky. "I'll go over and talk to them while you scatter the food around. The deer will be here soon— they know when it's feeding time!"

She walked over to the fence, and Rachel and Kirsty made their way slowly through the meadow toward the woods, scattering the deer feed as they went.

"My heart's thumping like crazy," said Kirsty in a whisper. "We're actually going to see real-life deer!"

RAINBOW magic™

Which Magical Fairies Have You Met?

- ❑ The Rainbow Fairies
- ❑ The Weather Fairies
- ❑ The Jewel Fairies
- ❑ The Pet Fairies
- ❑ The Dance Fairies
- ❑ The Music Fairies
- ❑ The Sports Fairies
- ❑ The Party Fairies
- ❑ The Ocean Fairies
- ❑ The Night Fairies
- ❑ The Magical Animal Fairies
- ❑ The Princess Fairies
- ❑ The Superstar Fairies
- ❑ The Fashion Fairies
- ❑ The Sugar & Spice Fairies
- ❑ The Earth Fairies
- ❑ The Magical Crafts Fairies

📖 SCHOLASTIC

Find all of your favorite fairy friends at
scholastic.com/rainbowmagic

HIT entertainment

RMFAIRY11

RAINBOW magic™

SPECIAL EDITION

Which Magical Fairies Have You Met?

3 stories in each one!

- ☐ Joy the Summer Vacation Fairy
- ☐ Holly the Christmas Fairy
- ☐ Kylie the Carnival Fairy
- ☐ Stella the Star Fairy
- ☐ Shannon the Ocean Fairy
- ☐ Trixie the Halloween Fairy
- ☐ Gabriella the Snow Kingdom Fairy
- ☐ Juliet the Valentine Fairy
- ☐ Mia the Bridesmaid Fairy
- ☐ Flora the Dress-Up Fairy
- ☐ Paige the Christmas Play Fairy
- ☐ Emma the Easter Fairy
- ☐ Cara the Camp Fairy
- ☐ Destiny the Rock Star Fairy
- ☐ Belle the Birthday Fairy
- ☐ Olympia the Games Fairy
- ☐ Selena the Sleepover Fairy
- ☐ Cheryl the Christmas Tree Fairy
- ☐ Florence the Friendship Fairy
- ☐ Lindsay the Luck Fairy
- ☐ Brianna the Tooth Fairy
- ☐ Autumn the Falling Leaves Fairy
- ☐ Keira the Movie Star Fairy
- ☐ Addison the April Fool's Day Fairy
- ☐ Bailey the Babysitter Fairy
- ☐ Natalie the Christmas Stocking Fairy
- ☐ Lila and Myla the Twins Fairies

■ SCHOLASTIC

Find all of your favorite fairy friends at
scholastic.com/rainbowmagic

HIT entertainment

RMSPECIAL14